For Aidan and William, my beloved Beans —KH

In memory of Little Granny, and our seaside adventures —CV

CANDLEWICK PRESS

Text copyright © 2022 by Karen Hesse ✺ Illustrations copyright © 2022 by Charlotte Voake ✺ All rights reserved. No part of this book may be reproduced, transmitted, or stored in an information retrieval system in any form or by any means, graphic, electronic, or mechanical, including photocopying, taping, and recording, without prior written permission from the publisher. ✺ First edition 2022 ✺ Library of Congress Catalog Card Number pending ✺ ISBN 978-1-5362-1404-8 ✺ This book was typeset in Gill Sans MT Pro. The illustrations were done in mixed media. ✺ Candlewick Press, 99 Dover Street, Somerville, Massachusetts 02144 www.candlewick.com ✺ Printed in Humen, Dongguan, China ✺ 22 23 24 25 26 27 APS 10 9 8 7 6 5 4 3 2 1

GRANNY
and
BEAN

illustrated by
KAREN HESSE CHARLOTTE VOAKE

Granny and Bean went walking one day
in the sand, by the sea, with the sky all gray.

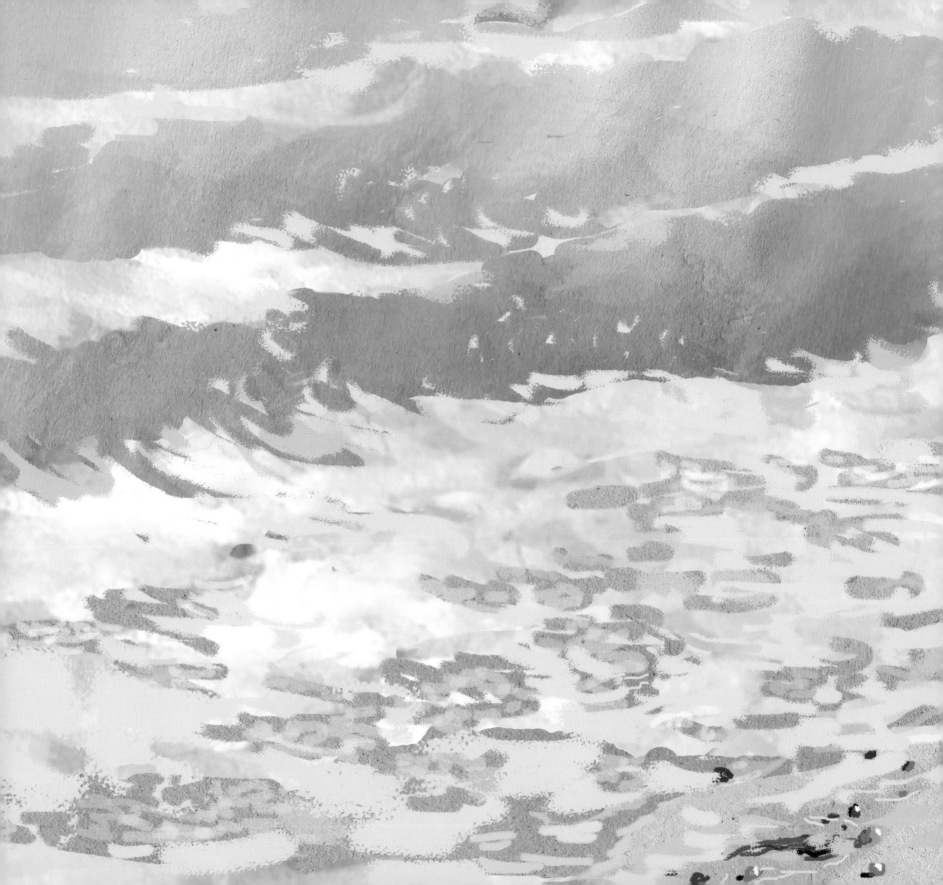

The wild waves crashed
and scuttered and reached
'til they wet Granny's toes
and made Bean screech.

Their laughter rose; full of joy, it spilled
'cross sand, through mist,
as the curlews trilled.

The herring gulls swooped.
Still they didn't head home.

They walked through the wind,
and the sand, and the foam,
their hats blowing free, their hair in a tumble,
but Granny and Bean, not once did they grumble.
Their cheeks chafed red and their hair dripping wet,
still Granny and Bean didn't head home yet.

They sang as they went.

They crouched to greet dogs.

They skirted a fence.

They leapt over logs.

Then the two settled down

somewhat out of the way

of the sand, and the sea, under skies all gray.

There Granny and Bean

shared a very nice tea.

And thus the two ended their day by the sea.

They sorted and kept their best shells and a stone.

And then, only then,
did they make their way home.